LITTLE ABE'S FIRST MUD SALE

Written by Susan J. Heil – Illustrated by Elva Hurst

Silver Line
PUBLISHING and BINDERY LLC

Little Abe's First Mud Sale

ISBN 978-0-692-40211-5

Printed in the USA

First Printing 2015

Publishing Services By:
  Silverline Publishing and Bindery LLC
  510 Sleepy Hollow Road, Lititz, PA 17543

Manufactured by Thomson-Shore, Dexter, MI (USA); RMA57DK87, April, 2015

Dedicated to all the volunteer fire companies of Lancaster County, Pennsylvania

"Do not neglect to do good and to share what you have, for such sacrifices are pleasing to God."

Hebrews 13:16

Foreword

Fire companies in Lancaster County, Pennsylvania are generally volunteer organizations. Fire company sales, mostly in the form of auctions, have been held by local volunteer fire companies since the 1960s. The money raised at the auctions help to support the funding of fire equipment, firemen training, and the maintenance of the firehouse facilities. The sales are generally held in the spring of the year during spring thaw, thus the name "mud sale." Many of the items are sold outside and others are sold inside the firehouse. It is not unusual for many auctioneers to simultaneously be selling both inside the firehouse and on the adjacent grounds. Local plain and English folk, as well as out-of-towners, flock to the mud sales for bargains, good food, camaraderie, and to get a good dose of the local atmosphere. Many Amish attend the sales and volunteer to help. The Amish are very active volunteers in the local fire companies and devote much of their time and talents to the sales and the daily functioning of the company.

Datt always said there are times when little ones should be seen and not heard. Waiting while his parents visited with friends, was one of those times. But little ears are big and hear much. Little Abraham, Abe for short, was minding Datt and patiently listening to him and Mam catching up with friends while on their weekly visit to town for groceries and such.

"Lizzie's not out of the woods yet, but the doctors said a few more days resting up should do the trick," replied Mrs. Fisher. Little Abe wondered what Lizzie was doing in the woods if she was feeling sickly.

"Let's hope that the storm last week was the onion snow. I'd like to start getting some planting done," added Datt. Abe whispered to his big brother Jake, "I didn't see any onions." Jake and older brother Ben got a big joke out of Abe's youthful curiosity. Abe didn't like when his brothers laughed at his almost unending questions. Maybe he should just not ask anymore questions.

"Remember to not spill the beans about the Ohio cousins coming for a visit," chimed in Mam as she headed for the buggy. "What beans?" whispered Little Abe to himself.

As the families said their good-byes, everyone agreed they would talk again next Saturday at the mud sale in Strasburg.

Abe decided to keep to himself his wonderment about why anyone would want to buy mud.

Mud was everywhere just now and rather a nuisance. Just last evening Mam commented that all this mud was for the birds. He guessed that birds must like mud just as much as Datt's pigs.

It was Friday evening before the mud sale, and it was making down with a light drizzle. Abe figured there would be plenty of mud for the sale if this kept up all night.

Datt broke the quiet of the evening with his announcement that it was time to head up the wooden stairs to bed and outen the lights quickly because morning would come way to soon. Datt said all the chores needed to be done swiftly in the morning, breakfast eaten, and everyone must be in the spring wagon and ready to go by 6:30 if they were to be at the mud sale in time for all the fun.

Abe, still being verhuddelt about the mud sale, said he thought maybe there would be too much mud for the sale if the drizzling didn't settle down. Jake called him a bobble and gave him a little push toward the stairs. Datt shouted to behave and Mam quietly said, "Gut notchen," as they all headed up the stairs to bed.

Everyone was wide awake before the roosters, and all were scurrying around just like the chickens.

Abe gathered the eggs and ran them into Mam, who was busy getting breakfast. She was frying up mush and scrambled eggs. She had some of yesterday's baked oatmeal she was reheating for Abe. He really liked that with fresh milk from Sophie, the cow. Mam knew everyone's favorites.

Abe's brothers, Jake and Sam, were tending the cows.

It was finally time to load up the spring wagon for the trip to the mud sale. Mam carefully carried out the pies she had baked, and Sam helped by loading the birdhouses Datt had made. Today they would donate the pies and birdhouses to the fire company for the auction.

"Kumm essa," called Mam and Becky rang
the bell to gather the family to breakfast.

After silent grace, Datt said to eat quickly and that he would see to it that they would all have some money for a donut when they got to the mud sale. This perked little Abe up. He figured that they must have more than mud at a mud sale! His brother Jake whispered to him that he hoped they would have whoopie pies. Mam told everyone that Susie King had made 20 dozen donuts herself this year and goodness only knows how many pies the ladies over on Bunker Hill made. Abe could only hope Susie made cream-filled donuts. Those were his favorite.

Mam thought it might be just a little muddy at the mud sale. She checked everyone for boots as they hopped up onto the wagon. Again, Little Abe had a question in his head. He wondered just how much mud fetches at a mud sale.

The ride to Strasburg was pleasant enough. The rains had stopped, the horse was cooperative, and the morning air was not too cold. It surely was going to be a great day for the family.

After finding a good place to unload the wagon, the boys all headed inside the fire hall for their donuts as Mam and the girls went to pick out good seats for the quilt auction. Datt had to find a place for the spring wagon and get the horse settled. Then Datt would find out in which tent he would be helping the auctioneer. He hoped he would be selling the handmade furniture and crafts.

ANTIQE
AUCTION
STARTS
HERE
9:00

Mam and the girls enjoyed looking at all the baked goods and the beautiful quilts on display. They hoped that many of the English would bid high on the quilts. The ladies worked hard all year long to make the quilts. They wanted their efforts to fetch lots of money for the fire company. It was a good day to visit too.

The girls soon ran off with friends to stand in groups to talk and giggle about the boys, and all the different clothing the English were wearing. They each had some extra money saved up for today to buy a trinket, candy, or maybe even a new purse from a vendor. Little Abe told his sister Sadie that he would like to have a big lollipop. Mam and her friends were just content to visit and admire the quilts.

Lunch time seemed to last all day. There were fresh cut french fries, soft pretzels, homemade ice cream, chicken corn soup, barbecued chicken, pulled pork sandwiches, and even hot dogs with sauerkraut.

Many of the older boys got into exciting games of football or corner ball in the afternoon. They worked hard all week and some fun was in order.

All the while as these wonderful things were going on, Little Abe was searching for the mud part of the sale. He saw antiques, carriages, groceries, plants, crafts, quilts, horses, hay, lawn tractors, brooms, bologna, cheese, and donuts, but no one selling mud.

He saw lots of muddy boots and shoes. He even followed a few, but they never led to where mud was being sold.

Abe grew tired of searching and joined a group of boys his age in a game of "King of the Mountain." He had a grand time, but expected Mam to be a little disappointed in his muddy clothes.

The day passed quickly and when it was time to go home, the whole family gathered at the spring wagon tired and happy. Datt had purchased a new horse that he planned to lead home. Mam was all smiles that a quilt she had helped to stitch brought $500. The girls each had a new key chain to hang on their purses. Brothers Sam and Ben each had a new straw hat for summer and a few bumps and bruises from their football game.

What did Little Abe have?

He had the muddiest boots of all, the dirtiest clothes of all, and a question he was bursting to ask. "Datt," he asked, "I couldn't see for looking. Where were they selling the mud?" Datt told him that it looked like he had found it and didn't even know it! "Just look at you son. You are taking home more mud than anyone else today, and you got it for free!" Little Abe looked down at his boots, his knees, and then his shirt.

"Ya, Datt, and it was a bargain, too!"

Author's Note

Amish children learn to speak Pennsylvania Dutch as their first language. They are exposed to little English in their community, at church, and at home. Pennsylvania Dutch is the dialect of the Amish which has its roots in the Old Country. The dialect originated with the German Lowland peasants in medieval times. The children get their first lessons in English when they attend school. It is very understandable that a young Amish child would have some confusion understanding everything that is being said.

An idiom is a phrase or expression that is understood in a given language. It is an expression, usually with two or more words, that means something other than the actual meaning of the words included in it. An idiom becomes difficult to understand because its meaning cannot always be inferred from the meanings of the words that make it up. Therefore, as in this story, misunderstandings can take place when learning a new language.

Corner Ball

Having 6 or 8 players, the playing field is formed by placing 3 children each at a corner to form a triangle if you have 6 players, or placing 4 children at bases to form a square if you have 8 players. The *Ins* take the bases and the *Outs* group themselves inside the triangle or square. The *Ins* pass the ball around the corners, throwing and catching until they see a good chance to hit one of the *Outs* grouped inside the boundaries. The ball is thrown at the *Outs*, and if the ball hits one, he is out of the game. If the *In* misses, he is out of the game. If one of the *Outs* in the center catches the ball, the ball is thrown back to a corner player with no score either way. When all of one side are put out of the game, the opposite side wins.

King of the Mountain

Having found a sizable hill or dirt mound, all the children scramble to the top to proclaim himself King of the Mountain. He then tries to maintain his position as the others try to overthrow him and thus become King.

Baked Oatmeal

1 cup brown sugar	1/2 cup melted butter
2 beaten eggs	3/4 tsp salt
1 cup milk	3 cups oatmeal
2 tsp baking powder	

Mix all ingredients together. Spread evenly in a 8" x 11" pan. Bake 30 min. at 350 degrees. Raisins, fresh seasonal fruit, or nuts can be added to the oatmeal before baking. This is a good breakfast, but served warm with ice cream also makes a tasty dessert.

Corn Meal Mush

Bring 1 1/2 cups of water with 1 tsp salt to a boil. Mix 1 cup of corn meal with 1 cup of cold water. Add the cold mixture to the hot water, but do not allow the liquid to boil while adding. Cook 10-20 minutes, stirring frequently to keep it smooth. This is delicious served hot with brown sugar, milk, or butter. Mush may also be put into a loaf pan and refrigerated. When solid, it may be fried in a very hot skillet until nice and brown. The fried mush is delicious served with maple or other table syrup. This is a filling, inexpensive farm breakfast.

Whoopie Pies-Original Chocolate

2 cups sugar
1 cup shortening
2 eggs
4 cups flour
1 cup baking cocoa

1 tsp vanilla
1 tsp salt
1 cup sour milk
2 tsp baking soda
1 cup hot water

Cream the sugar and shortening. Add eggs. Combine flour, cocoa, and salt and add the creamed mixture alternating with the sour milk. Add vanilla. Dissolve soda in hot water and add last, mixing well. Drop by rounded teaspoonfuls onto a cookie sheet. Bake at 400 degrees for 8-10 minutes. Sandwich two cookies with Whoopie Pie Filling. Makes 4 dozen whoopie pies.

Whoopie Pie Filling

2 egg whites, beaten
2 tsp vanilla
1 1/2 cups shortening

4 Tsp milk
4 cups confectioner's sugar

Mix together egg whites, milk, vanilla, and 2 cups of sugar. Then beat in shortening and remaining sugar. Spread the filling on the flat side of a cookie and top with another cookie to form the sandwich style whoopie pie.

Chicken Corn Soup

3-4 lbs stewing chicken	Salt for taste
2 qts of corn, fresh, frozen, or canned	Water
3-4 hardboiled eggs, diced	Pepper for taste
Pinch of saffron (optional)	Rivels (optional)
Chopped fresh parsley (optional)	

In a large kettle, cover chicken pieces with water. Salt to taste and cook until tender. Cool enough to easily remove chicken from the bones, dice, and return to the broth. Add corn, eggs, pepper, and saffron. Bring to a boil and add the rivels. Cook until the rivels are cooked through. Simmer until ready to serve.

Rivels

3/4 cup flour	1 egg

Put the flour in a bowl. Break in the egg and mix with a fork until dry and crumbly. Crumble the rivels into the boiling soup, stirring constantly until all the rival has been added.

Glossary

bobble	baby
kumm essa	come eat
Datt	father
English	non-Amish people
fetch	to bring (Fetch me a paper towel.) the cost (How much will it fetch?)
gut notchen	good night
Mam	mother
outen	turn off the light
werhuddelt	confused
wonderment	questioning
ya	yes